THIS IS ME!

BEHIND THESE EYES

Edited By Roseanna Caswell

First published in Great Britain in 2021 by:

YoungWriters® Est. 1991

Young Writers
Remus House
Coltsfoot Drive
Peterborough
PE2 9BF
Telephone: 01733 890066
Website: www.youngwriters.co.uk

All Rights Reserved
Book Design by Ashley Janson
© Copyright Contributors 2021
Softback ISBN 978-1-80015-686-9

Printed and bound in the UK by BookPrintingUK
Website: www.bookprintinguk.com
YB0489I

FOREWORD

For Young Writers' latest competition This Is Me, we asked primary school pupils to look inside themselves, to think about what makes them unique, and then write a poem about it! They rose to the challenge magnificently and the result is this fantastic collection of poems in a variety of poetic styles.

Here at Young Writers our aim is to encourage creativity in children and to inspire a love of the written word, so it's great to get such an amazing response, with some absolutely fantastic poems. It's important for children to focus on and celebrate themselves and this competition allowed them to write freely and honestly, celebrating what makes them great, expressing their hopes and fears, or simply writing about their favourite things. This Is Me gave them the power of words. The result is a collection of inspirational and moving poems that also showcase their creativity and writing ability.

I'd like to congratulate all the young poets in this anthology, I hope this inspires them to continue with their creative writing.

CONTENTS

Botwell House Catholic Primary School, Hayes

Olivia Mohan (11)	1
Hannah Jayeprabhu (10)	2
Ava Lueiro (11)	4
Kimberley Valenzuela-Porta (10)	6
Jessica Pope (10)	8
Mya Munro (10)	9
Elouise Lockley (10)	10
Sophia Borg (10)	11

Bysing Wood Primary School, Faversham

Ryan Bhagat (9)	12
Milana Volosin (8)	14
Nathan Olofintuade (8)	15
Naylen Folse (8)	16
Pollyanna Hubbard (8)	17
Millie Mortlock (8)	18
Sophie Agafon (8)	19
Owen Newman (8)	20
Tristan Bagshaw-Jesus (8)	21
Lottie Booker (8)	22
Marcus Galvan (8)	23
Logan Murch (8)	24

Cadle Primary School, Fforestfach

Mylie Witts (10)	25
Kai Lewis (10)	26
Damian Piekarski (11)	28
Cherry-Roxx Monaghan (10)	29
Layna Bowden (10)	30

Annaleecia Heard (10)	31
Charlie Taylor (8)	32
Lianna Ncube (10)	33

Craigellachie Primary School, Craigellachie

Maisie Smith (9)	34
Cole Anderson (11)	35
Madyson Mcdonald (10)	36
Lillieanne McDonald (10)	37
Lily Gordon (10)	38
Jayden Thompson (9)	39
Ailee Greig (11)	40
Isla Dawson (11)	41
Isla Macfadyen	42
Alfie Reid (10)	43
Kathryn Templeton (10)	44
Leo Gosling (11)	45

Haymoor Junior School, Poole

Jack Jenkins (10)	46
Olly Hill (9)	47
Georgia Whitfield (9)	48
Hannah Lisi (10)	50
Max Simpson (9)	51
Alexander Bartlett	52
Lily Martin (10)	53
Charlie Ellis-Andrews (9)	54
Holly Chissell (9)	55
Charlotte Wegman (9)	56
Violet Streeter (9)	57
Lili Shaw (10)	58
Sophie Bassil (9)	59
Billy Thain (9)	60

Archie Scott (10) — 61

High Cliff Academy, Newhaven

Alwyn Shati (10) — 62
Ben Hennessy (10) — 63
Macie Tookey (10) — 64
Lillymae Evans (9) — 65
Luca Mayo (9) — 66
Mona Cunningham (9) — 67
Mia Haines (9) — 68
Ruby Whatman (9) — 69
Lily Smith (8) — 70
Oscar Day (9) — 71
Oliver Brown (9) — 72
Sonny Foreman (9) — 73
Maxwell Bryant Tomkins (9) — 74
Ella Corbett (9) — 75
Lily-Rose Tidder (9) — 76
James Blackford (8) — 77
Mason Anderson (9) — 78
Matilda Clemens (9) — 79
Lola Whatman (8) — 80
Logan Knight (8) — 81
Sam (8) — 82
Ivy Pyke (9) — 83
Lila Balleste (9) — 84

Keith Primary School, Keith

Jamie Mearns (9) — 85
Riley Neish (9) — 86
Bethan Riach (9) — 88
Lexi Scott (9) — 90
Levi Dalton (9) — 91
Amelia Findlay (9) — 92
Kara McWilliam (8) — 93
Mollie Henderson (8) — 94
Danny Anderson (9) — 95
Callum Webster (8) — 96
Dylan Eyre (9) — 97
Holly George (8) — 98
Kenzie Laughton (8) — 99
Faye Stables (8) — 100

Brodyn Holmes (8) — 101
Blair McWilliam (9) — 102
Lacey Buchan (9) — 103
Callum Hogg (9) — 104
Indie Lewarne (9) — 105
Arran Bremner (8) — 106
Isaac Johnston (9) — 107
Ethan Lawson (9) — 108
Harry Spence (9) — 109
Harry Martin (8) — 110

Kensington Primary School, Manor Park

Vaishnavi Prakas Menon (9) — 111

Robert Bakewell Primary School, Loughborough

Chloe Campsall-Pollard (10) — 113
Alfie Moore (10) — 114
Callum Brown (10) — 116
Katie Beedham (10) — 118
Lewis Onions (11) — 120
Kera Anstee (11) — 121
Casey Smith (10) — 122
Mark Diamond (10) — 123
Holly Jarram (10) — 124
Zak Moore (10) — 125
Lara Sharma (10) — 126
Lola-Mae Wilson (10) — 127
Alfie Beale (10) — 128
Cohen Young (10) — 129
Sarah Vickers (10) — 130
Erin Gocer (10) — 131
Mason Hall (10) — 132
Kieran Dukes (10) — 133
Marc Best (10) — 134
Oliver Cunningham (10) — 135
Shreya Odedra (10) — 136
Archie Dalton (10) — 137
Kain Phillips (11) — 138
Stanley Birtles (10) — 139
Isobelle Eaglestone (10) — 140

Naseeb Ahmed (11)	141
Amari Jean-Pierre (10)	142
Oliver Mee (10)	143
Jacob Austen (10)	144
Lexi Tyler (10)	145
Callum Lievesley (10)	146
Lily Keith (11)	147

St James' CE Junior School, Barrow-In-Furness

Eloise Marrie Mullen (9)	148
Kasey-Mae Benson (8)	149
Kaydance-Bryn Parker-Ellis (9)	150
Patrick Moscrop (8)	151
Tulisa Briks (8)	152
Meisha Gower (9)	153
Annabella Dobby (8)	154
Oscar Doughty (8)	155
Daisie Evans (8)	156
David Tran (8)	157
Elsa Foster (8)	158
Alexa Thomas (8)	159
Kaiya Austin (8)	160
Blake Kirkby (8)	161
Jenson Stewart (8)	162
Jake Harris (8)	163
Tyler-Jenson Mould (8)	164
Daisy Alexander (8)	165
Rhys Purves (8)	166
Ava-Lilly Young (8)	167
Sam Lee-Mackenzie (8)	168

THE POEMS

The Future Me!

- **O** pen-minded. I am always open-minded because every time we have homework, I want to be the best and do my best
- **L** earning, for me, is important so that I can go to my dream school and have a lovely future
- **I** want to be a doctor, dentist or even an engineer, to be happy and to never give up because it can come true if you believe
- **V** igorous and brave to be ready to do anything like obstacle races or tournaments against people
- **I** am sometimes sad or angry but that doesn't stop me from being who I am
- **A** wesome and helpful to others when they are sad.

Olivia Mohan (11)
Botwell House Catholic Primary School, Hayes

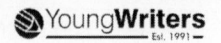

A Day At My School

T he morning is cheery as I leave quite quick
H astily passing the creaky school gate, I run with fear thinking I'm late
I am luckily early as I see my friends so I wave at my mum as I go to join them
S chool bell is ringing as I walk cheerily, talking to my friends about what's trending

I n the cloakroom, my apprehensive friend tells me she can't find her homework which was due today
S tartling with fear, she checks everywhere, only to find it at the bottom of her bag staring at her

M y friend sighed, as the teacher announced we were having maths then break
Y esterday, we practised lining up but today we were perfect so none of that now

L istening to the teacher, we scribbled down notes which were way too long

I could comprehend the complicated questions but some people couldn't so they made up excuses

F inally, lunch came, but it was over so quick, but I still enjoyed my delicious feast

E nding the day, it was topic and after the class book, we went home.

Hannah Jayeprabhu (10)
Botwell House Catholic Primary School, Hayes

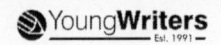

I'm As Free As A Bird

My name is Ava
And as my name suggests
I'm as free as a bird
Not caught up in anyone's nets

My hair is dark like a raven
And I have big hazel eyes
I am small like a robin
But I can soar to the skies

At school, I work hard
Like a woodpecker who tries
To be like an owl
Who is humble and wise

I dream to be an actress
Like a peacock, so proud
And to sing like a canary
To a friendly crowd

I want to dance ballet
Like a swan so graceful

And to play the violin
To make everyone joyful

My nest is so special
It is cosy with love
My family flock together
Like peaceful doves

This is me
Have you heard?
My name is Ava
And I'm as free as a bird.

Ava Lueiro (11)
Botwell House Catholic Primary School, Hayes

Questions, Questions, Questions!

When I'm stuck on what to do
I obviously don't know
But with the right questions
An answer will show
I toss and I turn
Not knowing what to fix
But with the right questions
I can learn some new tricks

When I'm struggling with math
Or even science or English
I can ask the right questions
And soon I can finish
I think and I think
About what I can do
But I can ask the right questions
And become as good as you

When quizzes make me queasy
I put my hand up and smile
Because asking the right questions
Is really worth your while
When I want to know about something
I let curiosity take the lead
If I ever had to name a very curious someone
I'd say that someone...
Would be me.

Kimberley Valenzuela-Porta (10)
Botwell House Catholic Primary School, Hayes

Princess Petal

Princess Petal is my majestic name
Don't worry, I'm extremely tame
My beautiful fur is very luxurious
And all my jokes are just hilarious
My stubby little feet are very pink
And my intelligent, huge brain helps me think
I munch and crunch on all my greens
I honestly think I'm healthier than you by all means
My black as midnight eyes stare into your soul
While my salmon-coloured nose sniffs my bowl
I am a unique guinea pig.

Jessica Pope (10)
Botwell House Catholic Primary School, Hayes

Mya

My name is Mya
Here I am in my full glory
I come from a generation of strong women
My soul is full of love and laughter
Which is given to the world with a glimpse of my smile
We are going through hard times
I wish I could spread more happiness and joy to all
I am compassionate and I love my family passionately
Glory be to the Lord, He watches over us and protects us
May our future be as bright as the shining stars pouring down upon us.

Mya Munro (10)
Botwell House Catholic Primary School, Hayes

Who Is My Idol?

She was born and raised in France, her home
And died of an illness that wasn't known
She followed every ideal of the Bible
Who is my idol?

Becoming a nun at a very young age
She was a good Christian who listen and engaged
She was The Little Flower, that was her title
Who is my idol?

She was a caring Carmelite
Who always shone as a light
Always acting like a saint and disciple
Who is my idol?

Elouise Lockley (10)
Botwell House Catholic Primary School, Hayes

What Animal Is It?

I am thinking of an animal
And it is a mammal
Some people say it is
The king of the jungle
And some say not
You wouldn't want to trouble it
Because you would be in a struggle
And it does not know how to juggle
What animal am I thinking of?

Answer: A lion.

Sophia Borg (10)
Botwell House Catholic Primary School, Hayes

To Make Me!

To make me, you will need:
A lot of kindness,
A pinch of happiness
A cheesy tomato pizza
A load of sports equipment
A bucket of water
A comfy sofa with a smart TV
And an extra-large bed
That's all you need

Now let's start cooking.
You need a pressure cooker
A pan and an oven
First, put all of the kindness in the pan
While it's cooking, add the pinch of happiness
And finally, the bucket of water
Next, you need to add the cheesy tomato pizza into the pressure cooker with all of the sports equipment,
Let it cook for a while
Then add the comfy sofa with a smart TV
Then finally, add the extra-large bed

Let it be cooked for good twenty minutes
Then put everything you have made in the oven
Cook it for an hour
When it's made... enjoy!

Ryan Bhagat (9)
Bysing Wood Primary School, Faversham

Recipe For Me

This is how to make me:

Add 1kg of sport
Add some chocolate
A dash of gymnastics

Now you need to:
Add some cookies and mix and bake
While stirring, add some purple
Pink, blue and yellow food colouring
And mix until it is bubbling
Add a pinch of sugar and mischief and pranks in
Spread it neatly over the baking paper
Cook it at 15°c for fifty-six minutes.
When in the oven, wait until it bubbles and splats
While there are five minutes left
Cartwheel around the kitchen.

Milana Volosin (8)
Bysing Wood Primary School, Faversham

Wonderful Me!

W onderful me wins in football
O n the top of most scored goals
N athan, Nathan, that's my name
D ancing is my favourite. I love a game
E ntering a competition, I'm always there
R eading, oh I love to do. If I'm not allowed, it isn't fair
F unny jokes I love to tell
U FOs I think they are real
L oads of sweets I love to eat

M y mum is the best
E lephants are my favourite animal because they are so cumbersome.

Nathan Olofintuade (8)
Bysing Wood Primary School, Faversham

This Is Me!

N ever eats beans
A lways eats pizza
Y ells at brother
L onely at the playground
E xcited for school
N ice and neat work

T ries to do times tables
O rigami master
M ini things are the best
M y dog is called Victor
Y ells at Victor

F ilthy on the field
O r clean on the playground
L ikes Automatas
S ad sometimes
E ntertains with a ukulele.

Naylen Folse (8)
Bysing Wood Primary School, Faversham

This Is Me

The time I'm happy, I'm in a good mood
Happily, I'll play with a toy at any time
I love warm hugs and films before bed
Suddenly, I'll go from mad to a cuddle mood

I love making art and crafting
Sweets are one of my favourite things
Even though they are not healthy

My favourite food is grapes
Erin is one of my favourite names
Because my best friend's name is Erin.

Pollyanna Hubbard (8)
Bysing Wood Primary School, Faversham

My Favourite

T his animal is my favourite because it is a bunny
H opping around eating lots of honey
I always laugh because they're funny
S ee them come out when it's sunny

I love bunnies because they are so fluffy
S ome bunnies' cheeks are so puffy

M y bunny and I are best friends
E very day, we play until the day ends.

Millie Mortlock (8)
Bysing Wood Primary School, Faversham

How I Was Made

First, add two buckets of kindness
Then add a teaspoon of smiles
A sprinkle of maths and mix gently
While mixing, add blue food colouring
Then add love, family, friends and pets
Put it in the oven until golden brown
Decorations are sprinkles of caring, chunks of me
Put in the oven for five minutes.
Enjoy me!

Sophie Agafon (8)
Bysing Wood Primary School, Faversham

My Favourite Animal

I'm a creature that climbs trees
And gets a bird's eye view
I eat bananas everywhere I go
In lakes, in rivers, having a bath
But beware of becoming my prey
I like to to go ooh and ah
With a tail that can curl
Can you guess?
No?

I'm a monkey.

Owen Newman (8)
Bysing Wood Primary School, Faversham

Me

T ristan is my name. I am eight
R eally friendly and kind to everyone
I love dinos
S porty and smart is what I am
T ake care of animals
A wesome cartoons make me laugh
N ewton is my dad's name.

Tristan Bagshaw-Jesus (8)
Bysing Wood Primary School, Faversham

My Favourite Animal

My favourite animal likes to neigh and play
It also likes to dance and prance
This animal likes to lurk as it gets to work
They like to do good as they normally would
Also, they run through the mud with a thud.

It is a horse.

Lottie Booker (8)
Bysing Wood Primary School, Faversham

Marcus Is Me

M y name is Marcus
A mazing at work
R obots are amazing
C hristmas is my favourite holiday
U mbrella is in my bag
S aturday is my favourite day because I have time to draw.

Marcus Galvan (8)
Bysing Wood Primary School, Faversham

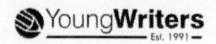

Me, Myself

You will need:
A nice cheesy pizza
A football player
A different gamer
A YouTube filmer
A reader
A nice cosy sleep
A phone
Some chocolate
And an Xbox
That makes me!

Logan Murch (8)
Bysing Wood Primary School, Faversham

This Is Me

When the summer breeze is gone and the heating is on
All I hear is bells and the only thing I see is bright lights
It makes me feel happy but only four days before I'm opening cards
With all the presents in the world lying at my feet
I never understood what makes me feel like this
With everything ticked off my birthday list
A high to the sky trophy after winning the race
The only thing that will stop me is the big ginormous cake
I'm still stocked up with candy
Knocking on doors, yelling, "Trick or treat!"
Hoping the only thing I get is sweet delicious treats
Summer is back, no more school
Sitting on a plane to go on holiday
To the famous Tenerife never failed me before
I come every year, what's one more?
All of this makes me, well, me
And doing it all again only ever motivates me.

Mylie Witts (10)
Cadle Primary School, Fforestfach

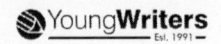

Black Blood

Blood is death but so is life
It's like hanging off of an infinite vine
Blood is red through a dead man's eye
But blood is black and that's no lie
A sheathed sword ready for battle
Preparing for a big rattle
Blood would be spilt
Swords would be broken
Another man getting killed in the ocean
Souls being salvaged for Man's evolution
Just like black blood, it's forever being stolen
The intelligence of man has brought nations
But only to war and was forever forgotten
Lives taken for gold and riches
But only we know better than this
Constant war, constant death
All for nothing but gold and wealth
Nothing is right, nothing is wrong
But all hope and safety is gone
Black blood spills and turns red
There is no way out of this ugly mess

War is war and forever will be
You can't stop black blood from spilling
It will be forever because of killings
We have no choice, we have no joy
Nothing stops war just live your own life.

Kai Lewis (10)
Cadle Primary School, Fforestfach

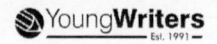

All About Me

I was born on the 21st September 2010
I was born in Singleton Hospital, Wales, UK
My mom and dad come from Poland
I can speak three languages; English, Welsh and Polish
I love to do creative things like drawing, writing, glueing and cutting
My hobbies are jumping on the trampoline,
Cooking, playing games and more
My favourite foods are Polish dumplings with cheese,
Large pizza with large pepperoni and extra cheese
And kotlet schabowy with ketchup
My favourite subjects are maths, English, history and science
My favourite drinks are water, lemonade,
Oranzada (Polish lemonade), orange juice and Pepsi
My talents are drawing, playing sports,
Making cardboard structures and cooking
My favourite sports are football and basketball.

Damian Piekarski (11)
Cadle Primary School, Fforestfach

Autumn Breeze

As summer goes out and autumn comes in
A cold breeze touches my feet and fills me up with joy
As I realise autumn is near
My smile shines out gleaming at the sun
The clouds fill up the sky
And the leaves turn red
I put on my costume that shimmers in the skylight
And I open my door and walk outside ready to trick or treat
I walk up to a big door and get ready for a sweet surprise, ready to be eaten

I wrote this because this is my favourite time of the year
I tell everyone my favourite month is October.

Cherry-Roxx Monaghan (10)
Cadle Primary School, Fforestfach

What Makes Me Happy

Going to the zoo is great fun
But we have to go when all the animal work is done

Ice cream on a hot summer's day
But the big bummer is that you have to pay

As summer starts to flee
Squirrels come out of the trees
They start to scavenge for food
As hibernation will begin soon

The woods are a place I like to relax
The centre of the woods I love, to be exact

I love how the fire dances
The crackling makes it more authentic.

Layna Bowden (10)
Cadle Primary School, Fforestfach

This Is A Poem All About Me

I have got nice, long, brown hair,
I have one dark blue eye and one light blue eye,
I have ten nice friends,
I'm really nice and kind,
I'm really good at drawing pictures and being creative,
I'm funny, hyper and moody,
I'm brave and lazy,
I'm gloomy and sneaky,
I'm hard-working and loving,
I'm sporty and confident,
I'm loyal and strong,
I'm open and silly,
I love wolves and I love reading.

Annaleecia Heard (10)
Cadle Primary School, Fforestfach

Best Of The Best

You can throw sticks at me
But I'm boxer tricks

I know how to fight and I do it right
I'm light on my feet
I go with the beat

We have the best of the best
The BKB

Together we win
All at Bomkings

With boxer tricks on our back
We will never slack.

Charlie Taylor (8)
Cadle Primary School, Fforestfach

This Is Me

A sprinkle of kindness
B rilliant
O utstanding
U nderstanding
T houghtful

M ature
E mboldened.

Lianna Ncube (10)
Cadle Primary School, Fforestfach

This Is Me

You will need:
A blanket-filled bedroom
A slab of chocolate
10lb of excitement and laziness
A pinch of anger
A dash of dog
A sprinkle of fish

Now you need to:
Add 10lb of excitement and laziness
Mix with a blanket-filled bedroom
Stir roughly while adding a slab of chocolate
Next, add a pinch of anger and a dash of dog
Spread the mixture neatly over a tray of baking paper
Bake until glazed and fun-filled stars can be seen
Sprinkle on happiness and pet fish and leave to cool.

Maisie Smith (9)
Craigellachie Primary School, Craigellachie

Tutorial For Cooking Me

To make me, you need:
Pepperoni pizza
An RGB lighting PC
A dash of valve index
And cat cookies

First, crush the cat cookies and put them in a bowl
Get the valve index and grate the headset
Then put this in the bowl
Stir rapidly until it's mixed
Now put the pizza in the bowl
And mash it until it looks like there's no pepperoni
Now add the PC and put it in the oven to cook

That's how you make me!

Cole Anderson (11)
Craigellachie Primary School, Craigellachie

This Is Me

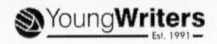

T here was a hula hoop on the floor
H ere I am playing Roblox
I was on the swing, then I went to see Patch
S oon we will go to a Halloween wedding

I s there a Roblox gift card
S us on Among Us

M any people ask if I'm Lillianne or Madyson
E njoy spending time with my family.

Madyson Mcdonald (10)
Craigellachie Primary School, Craigellachie

This Is Me

T he best player on Among Us
H elpful friend
I like Roblox
S ometimes I play football

I hate cucumber
S ome people think I'm funny

M any people think I'm brave
E njoy playing with new friends.

Lillieanne McDonald (10)
Craigellachie Primary School, Craigellachie

This Is Me

I simply don't like poetry
No clue why
I won't even give it a try
But every time I do
I might as well cry
I hate poetry
I still try...
But every time I do
I'm never late to cry
I still sometimes try
But every time I still do cry!

Lily Gordon (10)
Craigellachie Primary School, Craigellachie

This Is Me

Happy
Fun
Awesome
Smart
Passionate
Friendly
Scared
Helpful
Brown eyes
Brown hair

I like pizza
I like KFC
I like McDonald's
My favourite animal is a wolf
I like animals
My favourite sea animal is a shark.

Jayden Thompson (9)
Craigellachie Primary School, Craigellachie

This Is Me

T he most arty
H elpful friend
I hate tomatoes
S ometimes I go swimming

I like sports
S ome people think I'm brave

M any people say I'm good at drawing
E njoy crafting.

Ailee Greig (11)
Craigellachie Primary School, Craigellachie

This Is Me

A kennings poem

Animal lover
Horsey person
Messy person
Sporty lover
Arty lover
Strong person
Brave person
Funny lover
Maths person
Gaming person
Fun lover
Hard worker
Unhappy person
Kind person
Serious person.

Isla Dawson (11)
Craigellachie Primary School, Craigellachie

This Is Me

Art is my spark
I can put all my creativity
On to one page
But some paints go a bit faint
My best friend, Maisie
Said that I'm as amazing as a daisy
History is a mystery
But I think it's amazing
This is me.

Isla Macfadyen
Craigellachie Primary School, Craigellachie

This Is Me

A kennings poem

I am a...
Fun boy
Game player
Tennis player
Animal spotter
Curious man
Funny human
Deep sleeper
Friend maker
Artistic individual
Bird lover
Angry person
But most of all
A friend maker.

Alfie Reid (10)
Craigellachie Primary School, Craigellachie

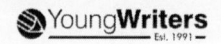

This Is Me
A kennings poem

I am a...
Bubbly artist
Flexible dancer
Axolotl lover
Independent cheerleader
Determined timer-hater
Kind music writer
Smart inspirer
But most importantly
An independent cheerleader.

Kathryn Templeton (10)
Craigellachie Primary School, Craigellachie

I Am A...
A kennings poem

Chatter, chatter
Me stopper
Game player
Fun starter
Bold jumper
Football fiend
Pasta lover
Curious kid
Silly maker
But most of all
A dog lover.

Leo Gosling (11)
Craigellachie Primary School, Craigellachie

Coding Me

Coding life takes much work
You'll need to add many lines of code
And coding blocks for it to work
Start off easy with your Sprite code
A ten-year-old boy with brown hair
And chocolate brown eyes
And red shirt mode
Add funny and caring function
With sensitivity and slight anxiety function
Boost brain function to increase intelligence
And don't forget to add some gumption
Enter taste sensation to love pizza and ice cream
And do not forget to add sound bites
Like laughter, talking and the odd scream
Add Sprite to background, in playground with friends
And add movement instructions to walk, run and bend
When you have finished, you should have a work of art
A loving, funny boy who is super smart.

Jack Jenkins (10)
Haymoor Junior School, Poole

All About Me

Olly Hill is my name
Playing football is my game
Score a goal and I'll be happy
I'm a fun, loveable, cheeky chappy
Liverpool is my team
Playing for them is my dream
I wear glasses on my face
They help me in a running race
One earring I like to wear
Plus I have gel in my hair
Buddy is my awesome dog
Out on my bike, he will follow and jog
Fish and chips are the best
They're even better with a guest
At home on my PS4, I can be found
Until dreaded bedtime comes around.

Olly Hill (9)
Haymoor Junior School, Poole

Emotional Weather

There was a girl
This girl, she felt all things
Tornadoes, storms and others
You might be thinking what do you mean?
I mean she felt stuff, bad stuff and good stuff

Here is the key
Tornado = overwhelmed and sad
Mist = anxious
Sun = happy
Snow = magic feeling
Rain = empty
Cloudy = dull
Hailing = missing something
Rainbow = hope
Storm = crazy

She feels these emotions all the time
But she doesn't know why she feels good sometimes

And she just can't explain why she always feels bad
So she wants to find out.
Georgia Whitfield (9)
Haymoor Junior School, Poole

Hannah

H elpful. I am helpful because I wash up and help clean the house
A rtistic. I enjoy making things, painting and being creative
N ice. I am nice because I let other people join in with my games and if someone is sad, I will help them
N ature lover. I love nature, going on walks, sitting outside or riding on a bike
A mbitious. If I make a mistake, I will try again to succeed
H onest. I will always be honest and tell the truth.

Hannah Lisi (10)
Haymoor Junior School, Poole

All About Animals

I love animals and insects
They make me happy, they make me smile
But when they're hurt, it makes me feel sad
I want to help when they're injured or frightened
I want to shout when I see them mistreated
Animals are awesome and so are we
Let's all learn to be kind
And live together in harmony.

Max Simpson (9)
Haymoor Junior School, Poole

Awesome Alexander

A wesome Alexander, that's me
L ego is my favourite thing
E xploring nature is another
X box is amazing
A nd TV and pizza too
N uts about Minecraft and dinosaurs
D igging for treasure
E xplosions and experiments
R unning wild and being me!

Alexander Bartlett
Haymoor Junior School, Poole

Lily

L is for lovely
I is for incredible
L is for lively
Y is for yay

M is for marvellous
A is for amazing
R is for reliable
T is for truthful
I is for inspiring
N is for noble.

Lily Martin (10)
Haymoor Junior School, Poole

This Is Me

C ooler than anyone
H onest as I can be
A s creative as you
R eading, I like
L ike school and football
I n PE, I like tennis
E very time I play football, I feel alive

I'm Charlie
This is me!

Charlie Ellis-Andrews (9)
Haymoor Junior School, Poole

The Life For Me

Arts, crafts and sewing
As creative as I can be
Warm sunny days and swimming
That's the life for me
Helpful, kind and caring
Is what you will see
But don't feed me
Peanut butter or mushrooms
Because they're yucky!

Holly Chissell (9)
Haymoor Junior School, Poole

Me

                C razy about craft
                H appy
                A good friend
     Unico **R** ns are my favourite
                L ots of fun
           Full **O** f joy
        I love **T** rampolining
Ready for any **T** hing
          Swe **E** ts are my favourite food.

Charlotte Wegman (9)
Haymoor Junior School, Poole

This Is Me

I am Violet, like the flower
Maybe I have a special power
I trampoline and come fabulous first
It makes me so excited I could burst
When I bounce I'm really trying
To get the feeling that I'm flying
I am a superstar.

Violet Streeter (9)
Haymoor Junior School, Poole

This Is Me!

T is for trustworthy
H is for honest
I is for inspiring
S is for sensible

I is for invincible
S is for smart

M is for mindful
E is for enjoyable.

Lili Shaw (10)
Haymoor Junior School, Poole

My Hopes And Dreams

At school, I daydream
That one day I will become a teacher
And teach my own class
I hope to be the fun teacher
The one that everyone will love
Hopefully, I will achieve my dreams
Be the best that I can be.

Sophie Bassil (9)
Haymoor Junior School, Poole

Billy

B lue is the colour of the ocean
I like pasta for my tea
L ego is my favourite toy
L ugging logs to make awesome dens
Y ummy chocolate brownie is the best.

Billy Thain (9)
Haymoor Junior School, Poole

Myself

- **A** is for animals
- **R** is for resilient
- **C** is for clever
- **H** is for honest
- **I** is for inspiring
- **E** is for entertaining.

Archie Scott (10)
Haymoor Junior School, Poole

This Is My Life!

This is me with a different life
And a different story
Every day, you should know
Different emotions come and go
One day, you're bound to be sad
But sometimes you are mad
We are different and not the same
So never ever feel shamed and lame
Always think before you say
Because some people think in a different way
But in the end, we're all the same in some kind of way
We all have a life and some are even blessed with a wife!

Alwyn Shati (10)
High Cliff Academy, Newhaven

Ingredients For Me

This is a poem all about me
It may sound like a baking recipe
But it is not as easy as baking a pie
You need a lot more to be a good guy

Take a squirt of happiness
And a glass of brightness
Grab two spoonfuls of shyness
And a pinch of anxiousness

Add three cups of funny,
Make sure it's runny!
Last but not least add a drop of unique
But you never know, this recipe may tweak.

Ben Hennessy (10)
High Cliff Academy, Newhaven

I Love Animals

I love animals, I don't know why
Even to the birds in the sky
Dogs are fluffy like a cloud
but ducks can be terribly loud
My favourite animal is a pet
Something I can go and get
Like a dog or even a cat
I'm not a fan of a scary bat
I love all animals small to large
But with a pet, I'm always in charge
Animals are important to mankind
So please, please, please keep that in mind.

Macie Tookey (10)
High Cliff Academy, Newhaven

Me And My Mum

My name is Lilly
And I'm very silly
My mum is in hospital
But she will always fight
She is very strong
And will always fight
But she might be upset in the night
My mum loves me so much
And I will always love her too
I love all my family too
I can't wait to see you
I will always love my friends
Because they're very nice.

Lillymae Evans (9)
High Cliff Academy, Newhaven

Luca Is My Name

L ike an ocean, my eyes are blue, my hair as blond as desert sand
U nder my shy exterior, I'm a normal nine-year-old boy who likes football and playing with my friends
C aring and kind is how I am, well, that's what my sisters think I am
A nd finally, when I grow up, I want to be an awesome, adventurous astronaut.

Luca Mayo (9)
High Cliff Academy, Newhaven

Mindful

M indful at all times, expecting what to do or to say
O nly if you knew how much I love you
T ogether forever, we make the world better as a team
H appy around each other, sometimes cry, sometimes laughter
E arthy and kind, you sacrifice your time
R emain calm and patient when chaos takes over.

Mona Cunningham (9)
High Cliff Academy, Newhaven

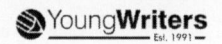

This Is My Friend, Cuddles

I have a friend
Whose name is Cuddles
Who likes to sing
He is much like me
He likes to defend
He finds it as a trend
He lends his help to children like you
So let's all say a big thank you
To our friend, Cuddles
He also says thank you
For being there by his side
In the hard times.

Mia Haines (9)
High Cliff Academy, Newhaven

Me Recipe

10,000g of love
A sprinkle of ginger hair
The peace from a ring-necked dove
A ladle full of care

A bowl encased in trust
A spoonful of joy
All this is a must
And just a touch of coy

Mix this all together
Everyone will see
Keep these forever
Because what comes out is me.

Ruby Whatman (9)
High Cliff Academy, Newhaven

My Life

T he best place is Disney
H ow is it so misty
I t is so amazing with horses
S lowly, they do courses

I t is a lovely day today
S he eats hay

M olly is a great amazing friend
E ven I have a phone so messages I can send.

Lily Smith (8)
High Cliff Academy, Newhaven

How To Bake Me!

First of all, a sprinkle of basketball, of course
Next, add a pinch of caring
Add sauce with kindness in
Stir it around but don't get weary

Add a bowl full of football next of all
Then a pinch of lovingness
Add two bowls of naughtiness at the mall
Stir it with comedy.

Oscar Day (9)
High Cliff Academy, Newhaven

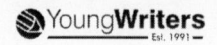

The Football Match

F rom Newhaven to Peacehaven
O n the muddy pitch
O liver, me, tripped someone up again
T aking the trophy home
B ut losing our next match
A nd getting another win
L ate to my next match
L osing the last match.

Oliver Brown (9)
High Cliff Academy, Newhaven

Collin's Rhyme

My name is Collin
I like vlogging
I love football
My life is as big as the sky
My ally is Bella
Today, I need to use an umbrella
Rain is a pain
What a shame
Dogs are cool
Just like you
Have a rest
Because you're the best.

Sonny Foreman (9)
High Cliff Academy, Newhaven

My Cat's Not A Pest

My cat is the best
My cat isn't a pest
My cat is fluffy and white
When he's scared
He will give you a great big bite
My cat's fur is a shade of ginger
At night, he sneaks around being a ninja

I love my cat and he loves me.

Maxwell Bryant Tomkins (9)
High Cliff Academy, Newhaven

The Singing

I like singing and not to dance
Always remember
That no matter how hard it gets
Someone has your back
Family, friends
Maybe even a pet or a teacher
So if you feel sad
You can always go to
Family, friends, pets or teachers.

Ella Corbett (9)
High Cliff Academy, Newhaven

My Dog

I have a little dog
She sounds like a hog
She looks so cute
And she has no boots
She gets wet feet
And she is crazy
I am the owner
I am cool
I love my dog
She is so cool
We jump in the pool.

Lily-Rose Tidder (9)
High Cliff Academy, Newhaven

The Riddle

Lives in the dark
Flies and some die
Also they're black
And the moon helps them shimmer to home
They love getting food from their mum
Dad feeds them
They love to go in dark, dark places.
What is it?

James Blackford (8)
High Cliff Academy, Newhaven

Me!

I'm Mason and I'm smart
And I have kindness at heart
Baking and basketball
Are some things I adore
I have got a brother
Who's really kind
But moans at me
If I forget to shut the door.

Mason Anderson (9)
High Cliff Academy, Newhaven

The Future Ahead

I look into the future
And I can see
What one day I can be
Someone that can save a life
Someone who can win a prize
I don't know because I'm still young
And my life has more to come.

Matilda Clemens (9)
High Cliff Academy, Newhaven

Lola W

L ove is my favourite
O hh I love half term
L ittle legs, little me
A teddy is all I need when I am sad

W atermelon is my favourite food.

Lola Whatman (8)
High Cliff Academy, Newhaven

Logan's Poem About Himself

L ove animals
O h I hope Christmas comes fast
G ood as I am I love my family
A fter school I love my family
N o one loves my family more than me.

Logan Knight (8)
High Cliff Academy, Newhaven

What Am I?

First one to space
I live in the jungle
I love to swing in the trees
Nearly extinct
Love to roam free
What am I?

Answer: A golden lion tamarin.

Sam (8)
High Cliff Academy, Newhaven

Amazing Me

I have a big imagination
I am kind to all the nation
I love all creatures
And all their cute features
Halloween is spooky
My friends and I are kooky.

Ivy Pyke (9)
High Cliff Academy, Newhaven

Lila's Story!

L ovely blue eyes that sparkle like the ocean
I love playing basketball
L aughing all the time
A rtistic and creative.

Lila Balleste (9)
High Cliff Academy, Newhaven

This Is Me!

To create me, you will need:
A sprinkle of pizza
A bucket of fidgets
A pinch of puppies
A spoonful of chatter
A jug of laziness
A brick of craziness
A hint of fun
A cup of bossiness

To make your Jamie Jaffa Cakes, you need to:
Put a jug of laziness in a bowl
Add a bucket of fidgets
Mix them together
Adda brick of craziness
Add a cup of bossiness
Fill the bowl with a spoonful of chatter
Put the oven on at 180°c
Then put the mix in the baking tray
Put it in the oven for twenty minutes
Take them out
Sprinkle some pizza, puppies and fun on top.

Jamie Mearns (9)
Keith Primary School, Keith

This Is Me

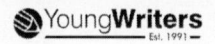

To make me, you will need:
Two dogs
One cat
A handful of hot dogs with ketchup
A splash of happiness
One teaspoon of kindness
A cup of friends
One bowl of walking
Raspberries and cream to decorate

To make your Riley Raspberry Cake:
Preheat the oven to 180°c
Put the two dogs and one cat in the bowl and stir
Add a handful of hot dogs with ketchup
Pour in a splash of happiness
Take a teaspoon of kindness and add to the batter
Slowly add a cup of friends
Beat in a bowl of walking until smooth
And divide between two cake tins
Bake for twenty-five minutes
Once cool, sandwich together

With raspberries and cream
And enjoy!
Riley Neish (9)
Keith Primary School, Keith

This Is Me!

To create me, you will need:
A tablespoon of rugby
A cup of kindness
A sprinkle of funny
A scoop of love
A dollop of happiness
A pinch of art

To make your Bethan Brownie Cake, you will need to:
Put the oven heat to 180°c
Get a bowl then get the spoon of rugby and add it in
Take a cup of kindness and put it in
Put the sprinkle of funny in
Put a scoop of love in
Put a dollop of happiness in
Last of all, put the art in
Then bake it
Let it cool

After it has cooled, decorate it
You will then have your Bethan Brownie Cake

This is me!

Bethan Riach (9)
Keith Primary School, Keith

This Is Me

To create me, you will need:
One hundred grams of my friends
A slab of art
A gram of eating snow
A kilogram of eating ice
A pink coloured bedroom
A splash of icing

To make your Lexi drizzle cake, you now need to:
Put the heat on to 180°c
Mix a gram of eating snow with a slab of art
Now add one hundred grams of my friends
Splat the eating ice in
Put the pink coloured bedroom in
And mix until it is smooth
Put in the oven for about fifteen to twenty minutes
Take it out and let it cool
Add the splash of icing

This is me!

Lexi Scott (9)
Keith Primary School, Keith

This Is Me

To create our Levi Chocolate Cake, you need:
A scattering of KFC
A pint of walking
A hint of art
A sprinkle of baking
Two pints of helping
Three sprinkles of drawing
And a gallon of hot chocolate

Now you need to mix a scattering of KFC
With a pint of walking to make a dough
Add a hint of art and a sprinkle of baking
And give it a good stir
Add two pints of helping and three sprinkles of drawing
Now you are ready to put the cake in the oven
Decorate with a gallon of hot chocolate and marshmallows
Enjoy with your family and friends.

Levi Dalton (9)
Keith Primary School, Keith

This Is Me

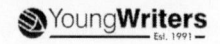

To create me, you will need:
A dash of laziness
A sprinkle of happiness
A spoonful of electronics
A teaspoon of hunger
A block of fun and mischief

To make your Amelia apple pie, you need to:
Add a dash of laziness
Pour a sprinkle of happiness
Mix a spoonful of electronics
Stir roughly while adding a teaspoon of hunger
Now add a block of fun and mischief
Spread the mix over a tray of baking paper
Cook until mischief-filled bubbles can be seen
Sprinkle on happiness and leave to cool down

This is me!

Amelia Findlay (9)
Keith Primary School, Keith

This Is Me!

To create me, you will need:
A jug full of animals
A pinch of electronics
A dash of clumsy
A slab of happiness
A sprinkle of trampoline
A teaspoon of friends
A spoonful of teddies
50 drops of family

To make your Kara Cake, you need to:
Pour a jug of animals
Mix a pinch of electronics
Next, a dash of clumsy
Stir in a slab of happiness
Now a sprinkle of trampoline
Spread a teaspoon of friends
Pour a spoonful of teddies
Cook until it rises
50 drops of family

This is me!

Kara McWilliam (8)
Keith Primary School, Keith

This Is Me!

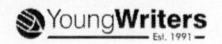

To create me, you will need:
A spoonful of messiness
Three jugs full of dogs
30 drops of drawing
A sprinkle of football
A slab of animals

To make your Mollie Muffins, you need to:
Get a bowl and put a spoonful of messiness into it
Add one jug of dogs, leave the rest for later
Now add two drops of drawing
Put a slab of animals in
Add the rest of the dogs in
Put it into the oven for twenty minutes
Take it out of the oven
Decorate with a sprinkle of football

This is me!

Mollie Henderson (8)
Keith Primary School, Keith

This Is Me!

To create me, you will need:
Ten gallons of football
One gallon of my friends
A slab of gaming
A jug of mischief
A teaspoon of tidy
A bag of fun

To make your Danny Doughnut, you will need to:
Add in ten gallons of football
Stir roughly a bit of gaming
Next, add a dash of laziness
Add some friends
Add a jug of mischief
Add a teaspoon of tidy
And a bag of fun
Put in the oven at 180°c for ten minutes
Mix it all together

This is me!

Danny Anderson (9)
Keith Primary School, Keith

This Is Me!

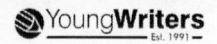

To create me, you will need:
A block of Lego
Ten gallons of football
A slab of scooters
A pound of Aberdeen FC
A jug of Sergio Ramos
A bowl of ice cream

To make your Callum Carrot Cake:
Chuck in a block of Lego into a bowl
Pour in a jug of Sergio Ramos
Scoop a bit of ice cream
Drop in ten gallons of football
Throw in a pound of Aberdeen FC
A big slob of scooters
Put in the oven at 166°c for two hours

This is me!

Callum Webster (8)
Keith Primary School, Keith

This Is Me

To create your Dylan date cake, you will need:
A bowl of friends and a pound of good humour
1lb of cheekiness mixed thoroughly
With hot dogs from Costco and 12lbs of PS4
With two lorry loads of sultana cookies

Now you need to add your friends
And good humour with cheekiness
Add the Costco hot dogs
Mix in the PS4
With two lorry loads of sultana cookies
Now bake
Stir the stuff and add icing
And sprinkles and a cherry on top.

Dylan Eyre (9)
Keith Primary School, Keith

This Is Me!

To create me, you will need:
A slab of laziness
A gallon of fun and mischief
A sprinkle of hunger
A jug of electronics
A block of pasta

To make a Holly Hot Pie, you need to:
Add in your gallon of fun and mischief
Then your slab of laziness
Now stir, whilst adding in your electronics
Now add your block of pasta
Then add a sprinkle of hunger
Now put it in the oven at 180°c
Leave to cool

This is me!

Holly George (8)
Keith Primary School, Keith

This Is Me

To create me, you will need:
A jug full of animals
A pinch of singing
A spoonful of friends
A dash of family
A cup of craziness

To make a Kenzie Cake, you will need:
A couple of stirs of craziness
Add a sprinkle of singing
Spread a bucket of friends
Now put a pinch of animals
Now mix in a kilogram of my family
Now put it on a green baking tray
Put it in the oven for two minutes

This is me!

Kenzie Laughton (8)
Keith Primary School, Keith

This Is Me!

To create me, you will need:
A dash of funny
A cup of swimming
A jug of playing the piano
A sprinkle of reading
A pinch of crazy

To make your Faye Cookies:
Add a cup of swimming and mix a pinch of crazy
Lightly stir a jug of playing the piano
Heat the oven at 180°c for ten minutes
Mix in a dash of funny and then mix a sprinkle of reading
Put in the oven for ten minutes
Then eat!

This is me!

Faye Stables (8)
Keith Primary School, Keith

This Is Me

To create me, you will need:
A dash of football
A sprinkle of biking
A jug of gaming
A pinch of chat
A teaspoon of staying up all night

To make your Brodyn Cake, you need to:
Add a dash of football in a bowl
Stir in a sprinkle of biking in the oven with the bowl
Add a jug of gaming on top
Mix a pinch of chat
Now finally add a teaspoon of staying up all night

This is me!

Brodyn Holmes (8)
Keith Primary School, Keith

This Is Me

To create me, you will need:
A slap of fun
A dash of hot pizza
10g of Celtic
A jug of Tae Kwondo

To make your Blair Brownie, you will need to:
Stir 10g of Celtic
Mix a lot of gaming
Put a dash of hot pizza
Heat the oven for one hour
Then take your Blair Brownies out of the oven
And pour a jug of Tae Kwondo
Lastly, add a sprinkle of funniness

This is me!

Blair McWilliam (9)
Keith Primary School, Keith

This Is Me

To make me, you will need:
Three sprinkles of kindness
A pinch of happiness
One pound of reading
15lb of computing
A handful of helpfulness
A sprinkle of fun
A pinch of Lego

To make the Lemon Lacey, you will need to:
Mix three sprinkles of kindness
Add a pinch of happiness and a pound of reading
Give them a good stir and put it in a tin
Cook for ten minutes.

Lacey Buchan (9)
Keith Primary School, Keith

This Is Me!

To create me, you will need:
A dash of craziness
A jug of laziness
A block of smartness
A spoonful of hunger
A lightning bolt of gaming

To make your Callum Chocolate Cake, you need to:
Add a dash of craziness and laziness
A block of smartness and hunger
A lightning bolt of gaming
Stir it all in a bowl and here you go

This is me!

Callum Hogg (9)
Keith Primary School, Keith

This Is Me

To create me, you will need:
A dash of playing
A splash of laziness
A kilogram of funniness
A pinch of chocolate

Now you need to mix the funniness with the laziness in a bowl
With the madness and a cute black rabbit
Now add the chocolate and put in a baking tray and put in the oven
Decorate with icing and a pound of drawing and enjoy with friends.

Indie Lewarne (9)
Keith Primary School, Keith

This Is Me

To create me, you will need:
A sprinkle of football
A gallon of laziness
A jug of craziness
A dash of baking
A pinch of hunger

To make your Arran Aero Cake:
Put a gallon of laziness
Add a dash of baking
Now add a sprinkle of football
Pour a jug of craziness
Stir a pinch of hunger
Now mix it all together

This is me!

Arran Bremner (8)
Keith Primary School, Keith

This Is Me Poem!

To create me, you will need:
A hint of cheekiness
10lbs of funny
10lbs of sporty
A sprinkle of being helpful
A 100lbs of cooking

To make the Ice Cream Isaac:
Mix everything carefully
Put 10lbs of funny and 10lbs of sporty in a tray
Add a glass of silliness and a glass of football
Put it in the freezer
Enjoy!

This is me!

Isaac Johnston (9)
Keith Primary School, Keith

This Is Me

To create me, you will need:
Ten gallons of gaming
A slab of football
A jug of laziness
A bag of fun
A pinch of craziness

To make your Ethan Eclairs, you need to:
Add ten gallons of gaming
A slab of football
Mix in a jug of laziness
Throw in a bag of fun
Chucking in a pinch of craziness
Heat the oven to 180°c
Enjoy!

Ethan Lawson (9)
Keith Primary School, Keith

This Is Me!

To make me, you will need:
A glass of cheekiness
A gallon of football fun crazy
Hot warm pizza
A handful of art
10lb of kindness

To make your Hungry Hippo Harry cake:
Add a pinch of cheekiness
Pour a gallon of football crazy fun
Add hot warm pizza
And mix them together
Bake them in the oven

This is me!

Harry Spence (9)
Keith Primary School, Keith

This Is Me

To make your Harry chocolate cake, you will need:
A dash of cooking
A splash of happiness
A pint of building

Now you need to put a dash of cooking
And a splash of happiness
Together in a bowl
Add the pint of building

This is me!

Harry Martin (8)
Keith Primary School, Keith

Rainbow Of Dreams

In my rainbow of dreams
I imagine being buried in a tub full of cotton candy
And have an enormous candy castle

In my rainbow of dreams
I imagine mountains surrounding the area
And it is raining sprinkles

In my rainbow of dreams
I imagine marshmallow penguins
Splashing and swimming
In a hot chocolate ocean
As I swim with them

In my rainbow of dreams
I imagine a cupcake trampoline
Which I jump on day and night
And when I wake up
I see that the sun is very bright

In my rainbow of dreams
I imagine a doughnut house

And when I come out
I become the doughnut fairy

In my rainbow of dreams
I imagine a rainbow chocolate auditorium
And when I went inside
I saw the most beautiful dance I've ever seen.

Vaishnavi Prakas Menon (9)
Kensington Primary School, Manor Park

All About Me

C hilled is the thing I do at home and I read
H annah is my best friend, without her, I feel lonely
L ily always makes me feel happy and very silly
O ver the hill is my fun play park
E mily is my friend, she makes me happy when she is around me

C hilled is who I am, it shows who I am
A wesome is all over me, we are all awesome
M aybe, sometimes I get sweets, sweets are my favourite
P asta is my favourite, I have it now and then
S illy, I'm sometimes a little bit silly
A ngry, sometimes I can get a little angry
L ola always helps me when I'm lonely
L ater in the week, I get a lovely takeaway.

Chloe Campsall-Pollard (10)
Robert Bakewell Primary School, Loughborough

All About Me

I play snooker, I play football
I will slip and slide in the game
People's smiles turn upside down
I'm as confident as an army man
Shooting a gun
And I run like my rabbit
I run all day, faster than a bullet
I like a challenge all day
All night, every day, every night
Even if I have to fight
Gaming is my fun
All day I play and play
I might play in the day
On my very fun game
I love my cars
More than chocolate bars
I collect them, I play with them
And I would like to design them,
Buy them and drive them
And customise them

When I buy a couple
Of one hundred thousand pound supercars.

Alfie Moore (10)
Robert Bakewell Primary School, Loughborough

What Do I Love?

I love so many things
Christmas, birthdays, everything
Going on holiday is so much fun
For me, for you, for everyone

Waterslides are the best
Even better than the rest
Takeaways, watching a movie
Opens up my chill

When I feel my happiness
I go all jumpy
I really don't like porridge
Because it's all lumpy

I love aeroplanes
They go *zoom!*
I like fireworks
When they go *boom!*

I enjoy playing football
It makes me very happy

I love my dog
Because he isn't snappy

I'm very smart
Don't you see
I am me!

Callum Brown (10)
Robert Bakewell Primary School, Loughborough

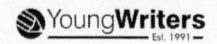

The Mystery Cat Hero

I saved a cat
By untrapping its tail
It was the opposite
Of old and frail
Its tail was trapped
In a metal fence
I felt so bad
So I had to help
I don't think I've ever been so glad
But sadly its tail couldn't be saved
If I would have left it
It would have got infected
And neglected
He could have died
But he is safe now
And oh his face
Is so adorable
I named him George
And we all love him
He is so cute

Even when he puts my TV on mute
I think he loves the buttons!

Katie Beedham (10)
Robert Bakewell Primary School, Loughborough

Jolly

Jolly lives in the brightest and most colourful places
He makes everyone have happy faces
When they free him, they let him play
Will they let Anger play someday?
Jolly is the kindest person ever
No one can possibly get better
If Jolly sees a bad emotion, he blows it away
It helps everyone have a brilliant day
He walks around with his chin up
He makes bad people look like muck
When Sadness sees Jolly, he gets scared
Somehow he runs as fast as a hare
Jolly can't have a bad day
Hopefully, he's here to stay.

Lewis Onions (11)
Robert Bakewell Primary School, Loughborough

Recipe For Me!

I need plenty of birthdays
They are the best
The cake is yummy
Although it's a mess

I am Albert Einstein
Extremely intelligent

Reading is fun
For me, for you, for everyone

A sprinkle of silly is all that I need
Though I am daft, I am cut out to lead

Endless fluffy pyjamas
They are outstanding

Fuzzy socks are warm
But they are way too prickly

Autumn all year round
Because blankets are so cosy

Lots of kindness
It makes everyone's day.

Kera Anstee (11)
Robert Bakewell Primary School, Loughborough

My Life

Compassionate and kind like a brown teddy bear
With a cherry-red bow tie
I love the colour yellow
But not more than marshmallows
Buttery popcorn at the fair
Dancing on the stall
I'm a curious one
Butterflies in my tummy
I'm lots of fun in games
November 16th is my favourite day
Not my birthday or my holiday
Carving pumpkins is my favourite
Winter's bite is nearly near
Autun leaves spinning and swirling around
Bye, bye summer, spring and autumn
Hello, winter.

Casey Smith (10)
Robert Bakewell Primary School, Loughborough

My Special Day

My birthday was cool and smooth
All the presents inside my room
Angels came out of the sky
Just to say hi
Then went back up high
In the light sky

All the presents I did like
But my favourite one was the bike
Family and friends had a great day
Celebrating my birthday
Everyone liked the cake
That my mum baked

I said goodbye to my loved ones
And thanked them for the gifts
That I couldn't count
Don't forget to come again
For another amazing day.

Mark Diamond (10)
Robert Bakewell Primary School, Loughborough

Messy Me

Messy is me
It always has been
It always will be
I always spill at least one drink
And I never put my glasses back in the sink

I am so, so messy
Just like my dog Jessy
We are twins
We never put anything back in the bins
Every day I will knock something onto the floor
And whack my ankle on the door
Messy is me
You won't change that
Even if you try it won't work!
When I smile, it feels like my mouth is running a mile!

Holly Jarram (10)
Robert Bakewell Primary School, Loughborough

Adventurous Me!

A ww, why can't I explore?
D ogs are cute and lovely
V ans are bad, from my experience anyway
E ating is the best
N ever hop into vans
T here are a lot of people who love rock climbing
U rgh! Why can't I use the zipline?
R olphes is my friend
O h! It's Halloween soon
U mbrellas keep you safe in the rain
S ome people love the night, but other people don't.

Zak Moore (10)
Robert Bakewell Primary School, Loughborough

Happy

Happy lives in the deepest places
Where Kindness plays on rides
But sometimes, happiness
Gets washed away by all the tides

Being the best out of them all
She loves playing ball
If Happy sees a bad emotion
She rubs down a special lotion
Which takes the bad away

When Happy sees Mad
She runs over Sad
Hoping to take away all the bad
If the wind blows her away
She will come back the next day.

Lara Sharma (10)
Robert Bakewell Primary School, Loughborough

Free Dancers

L ikes the adrenaline of the applauses
O nly the best of times are on the shimmering stage
L oving family will always be there cheering you on
A nd they might give you an amazing treat

M aybe butterflies will come to you
A mazingly makes you better
E ven if you think you're bad, you're probably as good as a professional dancer.

Lola-Mae Wilson (10)
Robert Bakewell Primary School, Loughborough

My Christmas Day

Christmas is a fun, jolly time
It's a great time to shine
Christmas lights, bright like the stars in the night
The glistening snow fell as the excited children ran to the snowy wishing well
The Christmas tree shone bright like Santa's sleigh at night
Rudolph's nose was as red as a candy cane that hung by a chain
The bauble jumped off the tree and landed with a bump.

Alfie Beale (10)
Robert Bakewell Primary School, Loughborough

Christmas Makes Me Happy

- **C** hristmas is the jolliest time of the year
- **H** olly and berries on the bush
- **R** oast dinner is my favourite
- **I** love opening presents
- **S** now falls on Christmas Day
- **T** insel on the tree, sparkles like a miracle
- **M** istletoe hanging up
- **A** mince pie fills my tummy
- **S** parkling Christmas lights, flashing fast and slow.

Cohen Young (10)
Robert Bakewell Primary School, Loughborough

What Makes Me Happy?

S wimming is so enjoyable
W hen I swim, I feel joyful like a dog getting treats
I 'm as kind as a cuddly koala
M y family is better than anything
M cDonald's after a long day of swimming
I am as friendly as a blanket on a cold day
N o one loves swimming more than I do
G ingerbread men at Christmas time.

Sarah Vickers (10)
Robert Bakewell Primary School, Loughborough

What Emotion Am I?

Too many questions in my head
I have a wild imagination
That cannot even be read
My eyebrows are frowning
But I still understand
Is it maths or is it English?
I question myself too much
That I can't stay on topic
What's that in my pocket?
Oh, I really need to fix my tie
Now... What emotion am I?

Answer: Confused/curious.

Erin Gocer (10)
Robert Bakewell Primary School, Loughborough

When Is It Halloween?

H alloween is the best holiday
A ll I see are amazing costumes
L uxury treats we get from you
L ovely costumes we all wear
O ctober is the month of Halloween
W hen it's Halloween, we get sweets
E veryone wears costumes
E veryone loves candy
N o one loves Halloween more than me!

Mason Hall (10)
Robert Bakewell Primary School, Loughborough

All About Me

C hristmas is my favourite season
H appy is the best feeling in the world
R ed spreads Christmas cheer
I love making snowmen
S ummer will soon be here
T homas is my middle name
M aths is the best subject
A rithmetic is the easiest for me
S cience is one of my favourite subjects.

Kieran Dukes (10)
Robert Bakewell Primary School, Loughborough

All About Me

My life is as happy as a monkey swinging on a tree
My anger is as calm as a gorilla eating a banana
I am not as smart as a scientist
I am as friendly as a chipmunk playing football
I am as chilled as an excited dog catching a ball
I am not like a worried cat
I am as kind as a loyal lion.

Marc Best (10)
Robert Bakewell Primary School, Loughborough

Sports

S unny times are the best for me to do some sports
P eople can play sports indoors or outdoors
O utside is best for sports in my opinion
R arely do I get injured in games I play
T oday, I might play basketball
S ometimes you could be really hot and sweaty.

Oliver Cunningham (10)
Robert Bakewell Primary School, Loughborough

Who I Am!

I'm as curious as a snake
And as fun as a tub of slime
I'm as confident as a peacock
And as chilled as an ice lolly
I'm as calm as a sleeping cat
And as chatty as a parrot
I am unique because I have two fingers
And that will never stop me

This is who I am!

Shreya Odedra (10)
Robert Bakewell Primary School, Loughborough

Anxious

I wait in the car
Going afar
Looking at the screen ahead
I'm feeling sick
And my phlegm's getting thick
It always gives me butterflies
When I look at my SATs
The same as well
When I think of rats
Anxious, I am
Unready to meet
My defeat.

Archie Dalton (10)
Robert Bakewell Primary School, Loughborough

October

O ptimism, Halloween is coming
C ourage is needed when it's scary
T rick or treating with my family
O n a dark and breezy night
B rother is causing trouble
E verybody likes sweets
R oll on Bonfire Night, when October ends.

Kain Phillips (11)
Robert Bakewell Primary School, Loughborough

About Me

A ll about me
B old people are strong
O ur life is a once in a lifetime opportunity
U nderstandable friends are great
T esting myself for great chances

M ixed feelings aren't very good
E veryone has a heart.

Stanley Birtles (10)
Robert Bakewell Primary School, Loughborough

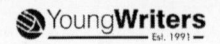

Isobelle

I am so angry
S ometimes I'm passionate
O ften I'm sad
B ut I am curious
E very now and then, I'm adventurous
L ike, I'm so worried
L ater, I will be excited
E very day, I am sporty.

Isobelle Eaglestone (10)
Robert Bakewell Primary School, Loughborough

Myself

M y life is a happy and peaceful life
Y awning every night and brawling in my dreams
S miling as always in all the photos
E ating food like fruit
L ife is mine, like a flying knife
F ight me now, then I'll bite you.

Naseeb Ahmed (11)
Robert Bakewell Primary School, Loughborough

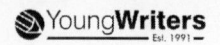

The Great Sports

I play football because I run
And that's how I enjoy myself because it is fun
If someone slide tackles me
I will push them
And if I push that means anger is here
It will shout out, it will fight
It goes on until happiness comes.

Amari Jean-Pierre (10)
Robert Bakewell Primary School, Loughborough

The Midnight Sky

O ver the hill, I lay still
L ike a rock in water
I think to myself
V ery still, I look up at the stars
E very night, I do the same thing
R eading my thoughts, I smile.

Oliver Mee (10)
Robert Bakewell Primary School, Loughborough

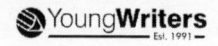

What Am I?

I'm as bright as the sun
I sparkle like a light
I only come out at night
I share the sky with the dark night
I am very bright
What am I?

Answer: A bright star, just like you!

Jacob Austen (10)
Robert Bakewell Primary School, Loughborough

Honest Me!

Being honest is helping people
With their lives
Messiness is making
My life hard
I'm as chilled
As a pill
And like Phil
My cat sleeping
Is as kind as a mouse.

Lexi Tyler (10)
Robert Bakewell Primary School, Loughborough

What Animal Am I?

I have four legs
I'm a vertebrate
You can keep me as a pet
I have fur
I can be dark and light colours
I can run very fast
I have small legs

I am a rabbit.

Callum Lievesley (10)
Robert Bakewell Primary School, Loughborough

Fun And Games

Fun like the sun
Life runs the reins
All fun and games
Some people find it annoying
Which is such a shame
We don't want fame
We want to play games!

Lily Keith (11)
Robert Bakewell Primary School, Loughborough

This Is Me

E xcellent Eloise is great at crafting
L ikes to dance and sing and definitely smile
O h, I absolutely love dogs
I cy snow cones, I love them as a nice summer treat
S o my favourite colour is purple
E lectrifying singing Eloise

M y brother likes to play with cars
U nmute the music, let's party!
L ovely Eloise chats to her classmates
L oves puppies and other cute animals
E loise loves to play with her brother
N ice Eloise hugs her mum before she goes to sleep.

Eloise Marrie Mullen (9)
St James' CE Junior School, Barrow-In-Furness

This Is Me!

K asey is weird but can be funny sometimes and loves KFC, arcades with claw machines and the game Crossy Road

A wesome at crafting and drawing. My favourite colours are purple, yellow and blue

S ometimes I get obsessed with food and always want food all the time. I like burritos, chicken nuggets, fries, chicken dippers and pizza. I love food!

E at chicken nuggets with chips. They are amazing

Y ummy chicken nuggets. I also like blowing bubbles.

Kasey-Mae Benson (8)
St James' CE Junior School, Barrow-In-Furness

Kaydance

K aleb is my brother's name. He is in year eleven
A nd Kaydance likes playing with her wonderful friends at the park
Y ippee! She's getting a fish
D isney, she had lots of great films that she watches
A s awesomely fast as a cheetah
N obody dislikes her or her family
C ats are her second favourite animal
E loise is her best friend.

Kaydance-Bryn Parker-Ellis (9)
St James' CE Junior School, Barrow-In-Furness

All About Patrick

- **P** atrick is tall and I am a good footballer and love McDonald's
- **A** n amazing, fantastic footballer who is a super shooter
- **T** all as a tree and he is as fast as Jenson
- **R** acing around in the playground and playing
- **I** love to play at the park to play football
- **C** ute and handsome
- **K** ick the football and shoot a goal.

Patrick Moscrop (8)
St James' CE Junior School, Barrow-In-Furness

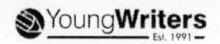

Tulisa

T elevision is my favourite and I like watching Peppa Pig and PAW Patrol
U ses glasses to see but then got new ones
L ove going to the beach and making sandcastles
I n our house, playing in our bedroom with my brothers and sisters
S isters are good because they make me smile
A lways smiling.

Tulisa Briks (8)
St James' CE Junior School, Barrow-In-Furness

This Is About Me!

M cDonald's is my favourite food
E very time I go there, I get chicken nuggets and chips
I love my bed because it is super comfy
S he is so cool, she likes to ride her bike
H er hobby is knitting, she is making a scarf for her teddy
A phone keeps me occupied because I play my games.

Meisha Gower (9)
St James' CE Junior School, Barrow-In-Furness

This Is Me

A pples are my favourite
N ever seen a unicorn
N othing excites me more than gymnastics
A lways smiling
B eing kind
E very day, I wear my glasses
L ove playing Cave Club dolls
L ove lasagne
A nd meatballs.

Annabella Dobby (8)
St James' CE Junior School, Barrow-In-Furness

Oscar

- **O** nly likes Liverpool and Celtic football club
- **S** ometimes I play basketball with my friends
- **C** hooses to play on iPad instead of PS5 because it has Roblox
- **A** lways watching telly on YouTube
- **R** eally likes Rocket League and has got to level fourteen.

Oscar Doughty (8)
St James' CE Junior School, Barrow-In-Furness

This Is Me

D oes not like the rain but likes the sun
A lways likes to watch Chad and V on YouTube
I s good at Minecraft
S ister's show me how to play new games
I go to swimming lessons
E ventually, I will be in stage three in swimming.

Daisie Evans (8)
St James' CE Junior School, Barrow-In-Furness

All About David

D avid likes sweets and chocolate
A mazing David likes playing cool, awesome games
V ery good at maths and English
I like to eat lots of food. My favourite food is eggs
D avid is a very cool, awesome person!

David Tran (8)
St James' CE Junior School, Barrow-In-Furness

This Is Me

E lsa is imaginative and likes to read interesting fairytales
L ovely lollipops are my favourite things to lick
S uper music is what I like to hear
A mazing stars is what I like to look at when it is night-time.

Elsa Foster (8)
St James' CE Junior School, Barrow-In-Furness

All About Me

A lexa likes adorable dogs
L ollipops are tasty, that's why I like them
E xtra good at running
X ylophones are one of my favourite instruments
A lexa loves her family and friends.

Alexa Thomas (8)
St James' CE Junior School, Barrow-In-Furness

This Is Me

K aiya has seven pets
A nd my pets' names are Rosie, Diego, Peanut, Wodels, Daisy, Snowball and Sky
I like dogs
Y oung Kaiya is cute
A nd my name is Kaiya. What's your name?

Kaiya Austin (8)
St James' CE Junior School, Barrow-In-Furness

Blake The Cake

B lake likes Ronaldo and Messi
L akes are my favourite thing to swim in
A monkey showed up at my house
K ing Blake likes eating his birthday cake
E veryone parties around the cake.

Blake Kirkby (8)
St James' CE Junior School, Barrow-In-Furness

This Is Me

J enson is a great runner
E ggy bread is my favourite
N ot a negative person
S omeone helps me, I help them
O h my, I am so good at football
N ot naughty, I'm good.

Jenson Stewart (8)
St James' CE Junior School, Barrow-In-Furness

This Is Me

J ake is a fabulous football player that skills everyone
A mazing at long shots
K icking front and back, scoring constantly
E verybody engaged in the match, jumping around.

Jake Harris (8)
St James' CE Junior School, Barrow-In-Furness

This Is Me

T he amazing boy, Tyler
Y ou and me are so cool
L oves gaming, such an amazing gamer
E xcept or when he plays Fortnite
R hys is a good friend to Tyler.

Tyler-Jenson Mould (8)
St James' CE Junior School, Barrow-In-Furness

This Is Me

D aisy loves picking up chickens
A mazing animal carer
I love big animals
S ee animals every day
Y ou will love to see the chickens as much as I do.

Daisy Alexander (8)
St James' CE Junior School, Barrow-In-Furness

This Is Me

R hys is a skilful, speedy footballer
H andsome and amazing
Y ou, my friend, are very kind
S o good at Minecraft. I can speed run in thirty minutes.

Rhys Purves (8)
St James' CE Junior School, Barrow-In-Furness

This Is Me!

A va loves axolotls, amazing, awesome animals
V ideos about amazing, funny, cute cats and dogs
A va loves pizza and cookies.

Ava-Lilly Young (8)
St James' CE Junior School, Barrow-In-Furness

Sam

S am loves playing on his Xbox
A mazing Sam likes playing basketball
M agnificent at playing football.

Sam Lee-Mackenzie (8)
St James' CE Junior School, Barrow-In-Furness

YoungWriters® Est. 1991

YOUNG WRITERS INFORMATION

We hope you have enjoyed reading this book – and that you will continue to in the coming years.

If you're the parent or family member of an enthusiastic poet or story writer, do visit our website www.youngwriters.co.uk/subscribe and sign up to receive news, competitions, writing challenges and tips, activities and much, much more! There's lots to keep budding writers motivated!

If you would like to order further copies of this book, or any of our other titles, then please give us a call or order via your online account.

Young Writers
Remus House
Coltsfoot Drive
Peterborough
PE2 9BF
(01733) 890066
info@youngwriters.co.uk

Join in the conversation!
Tips, news, giveaways and much more!

 YoungWritersUK   YoungWritersCW   youngwriterscw